# SEA WATCH

## A BOOK OF POETRY

JANE YOLEN

*illustrated by* TED LEWIN

*Philomel Books    New York*

Library of Congress Cataloging-in-Publication Data
Yolen, Jane.   Sea watch / Jane Yolen; illustrations by Ted Lewin.   p.   cm.
Summary: A collection of poems describing a variety of sea creatures and their activities.
1. Marine fauna—Juvenile poetry. 2. Children's poetry, American.
[1. Marine animals—Poetry. 2. American poetry.]   I. Lewin, Ted, ill.   II. Title.
PS3575.043S43   1996   811*.54—dc20   94-32533 CIP AC
ISBN 0-399-22734-2

1   3   5   7   9   10   8   6   4   2

First Impression

*For Patty and Bob MacLachlan,*
*who sometimes live near the sea*

*—J. Y.*

*To Capt. Don Stewart*

*—T. L.*

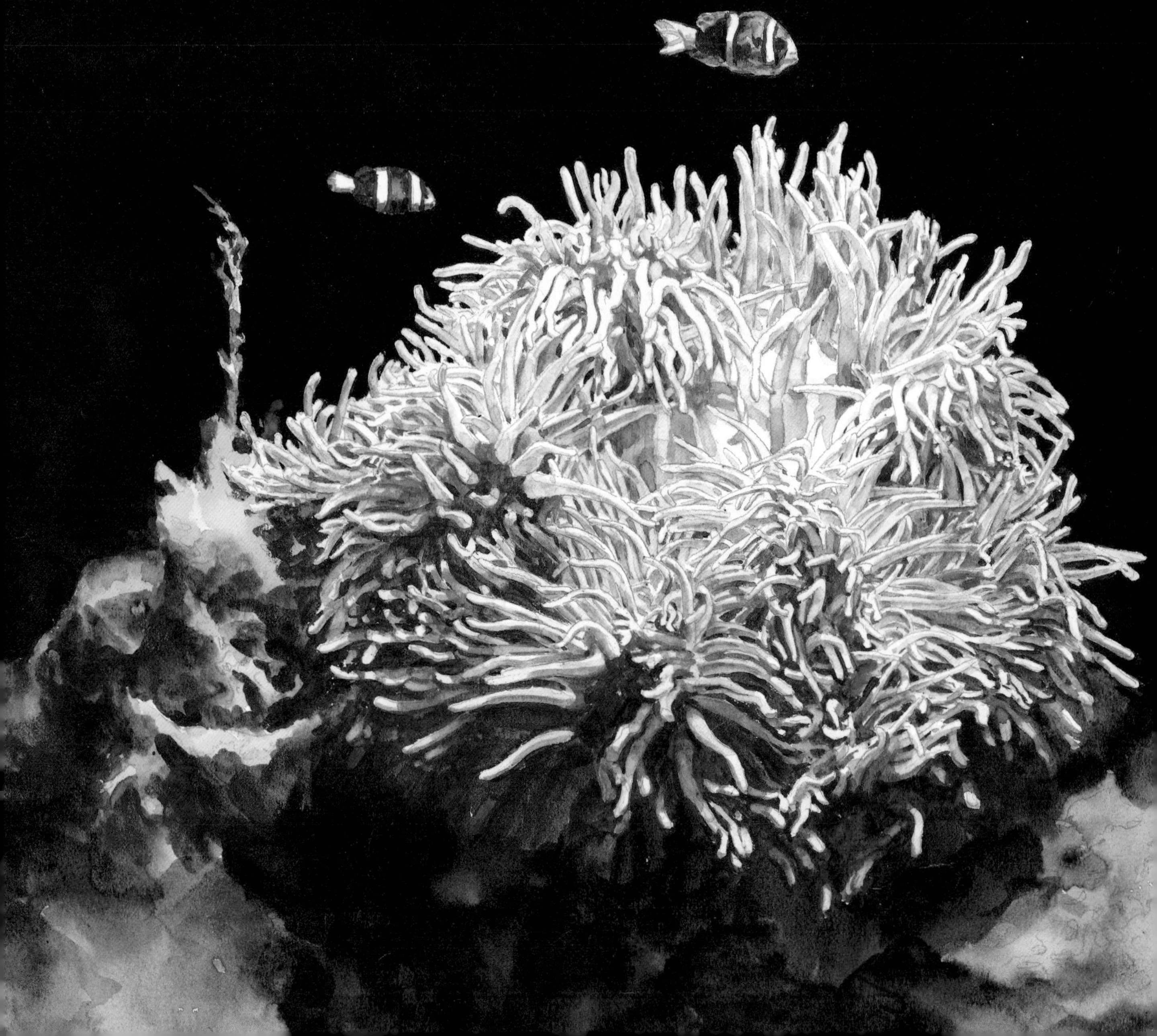

## ANEMONE

A flower with no smell,
A fisher with no line,
A trapper with no lure
Who, mouthless, still can dine.

A rider without legs,
A killer without hands
Who, silent, waits a lifetime
On shifting sea-soft sands.

## THE GRUNION

A sliver of silver moon,
A California strand,
A thousand thousand wriggling fish
Upon the dark wet sand.

A thousand thousand fish
Upon the beaches ride,
Their only light the silvered moon,
Their compass but the tide.

## FATHER SEAHORSE

His belly pouch,
like a Snuggli of skin,
enfolds the eggs
til the young fish hatch,
swimming away
into the ever green fields
of the sea.

## SEA CANARY—BELUGA

We heard her, white and weary,
singing a last song,
her whistle following us
into the night.
Did she sing of her young
still brown behind her?
Or of the bottoms of waves
made light by the moon?
Or did she sing her death,
the harps still heavy in her bones,
pulling her toward the air
and the long dark shanks of our hold?

## PAPER NAUTILUS

Both keel and sail,
Her paper-thin shell

Like the *Argo* of old,
A boat well-held

By the sailors' arms.
She sets the terms

For her open-sea life.
Her young are safe

Within the shell.
She sails it well.

## WARNING: SHARKS

Beware the bear-trap jaw,
the teeth,
another five sets set
beneath the gum,
and that vast stomach full
of things such long immersion's
dulled:
a keg of nails,
a ragged coat,
a boat's dark anchor,
a child's white shoe,
a heavy brass-bound antique trunk.
All the things that man can make,
from ancient seas the shark can take.

## THE CRAB

What do we know of direction?
The sea invites but four:
forward and back,
the swift arithmetic of fin and tail;
up and down,
the careful ballast of body and weight.

Yet with a mathematics all its own,
the crab clowns
into a fifth dimension,
skittering sideways
into the patient calculations of the sea.

## PORTUGUESE MAN-OF-WAR

The riddler asks:
Where comes one out of many?
In what land are tasks so sure?
Workers who only hunt,
Hunters who only catch,
Catchers who only lay eggs,
And those whose work is to eat the food.
There is no city,
There is no state,
There is no empire so vast
That so divides its workers' tasks.
There is but in the deepest seas
The answer—in the colonies
Of man-of-war.

## LEATHERBACK TURTLE

There are two skylines here:
the night-black mangroves
and the rough-ridged mound,
like a moving mountain,
as the leatherback ploughs
its certain course
between the boat and shore.

## PACIFIC SALMON

Bear teaser,
falls jumper,
autumn star
flashing silver
til the spawning grounds
prove your eclipse.

## SEA OTTER

He speaks in tongues,
one for each mood:
a grunting when the food is good;
a whistle or whine
past dinnertime;
a hiss of warning
or of fright;
a growl if caught;
a coo at night
to woo a mate,
to soothe the young,
or when a coat
needs cleaning up;

and a horrid half-mile scream
at the killing
of a pup.

## OCTOPUS

One arm for walking,
Two arms for stalking,
Three arms for gripping,
Four against slipping,
Five arms for speeding,
Six arms for feeding,

## BARRACUDA

A swimming saw
With razored teeth,
Predacious jaw,
Deals death beneath

              the warm seas.

A restless eye,
A reckless leap,
The small fish die
Down in the deep
and warm seas.

Alert and lone
*Picuda* waits;
His hungers hone
The fishes' fates
in warm seas.

## KILLER WHALES

Five and fifty in our pack,
White below and topside black.
Put your babe upon your back
Or he is ours today.

See us coming, tail and fin,
We devour dolphin kin,
Eat them up, both flesh and skin,
And they are ours today.

Knifing through the ocean's blue,
Five and fifty after you,
Nothing's left when we are through,
And you are ours today.

# SEA WATCH NOTES

*Page 5*  ANEMONES, though they look like flowers, are hollow, jellylike animals belonging to the same group as jellyfish and corals. What looks like petals are actually tentacles equipped with stinging cells. With these cells the anemones poison their prey.

*Page 7*  GRUNION: Of the many thousands of fish in the oceans, only the grunion lays its eggs on land. They arrive at night on the beaches of Southern California when peak tides are beginning to ebb and leap out of the water onto the sand. They mate, the females lay their eggs, and then they catch the ebbing waves back. The eggs hatch just when the next high tide arrives to carry the baby grunion into the water. What timing!

*Page 8*  SEAHORSE is a small marine fish with a horselike appearance in the head and arched neck. The female seahorse deposits her eggs in a pouch under the male's tail and he then broods the young until they hatch.

*Page 11*  BELUGA or white whale is related to the narwhale. Because of their high-pitched chirping sounds, belugas were called "sea canaries" by sailors who hunted them with "harps" or harpoons. Belugas are extremely social animals, traveling in packs, and often have been observed helping out one another at times of illness or when they are being hunted.

*Page 12*  PAPER NAUTILUS has a fragile shell much sought after by collectors. Large flaps, or membranes, are part of the shell and they cradle the nautilus eggs until the eggs are ready to hatch out into the open sea. The Latin name for this kind of nautilus is "Argonauta," referring to the sailors, the Argonauts, who sailed with the great mythic hero Jason on his ship, the *Argo*, when they went adventuring after the Golden Fleece.

*Page 15*  SHARKS have been around for more than 300 million years. In fact, there were sharks before there were dinosaurs. A shark's huge jaws are lined with razor-sharp teeth but are not set into the bone, so they can fall out rather easily. Of course, sharks have four or five rows of spare teeth, so any that fall out can be just as easily replaced. Sharks have been known to swallow things they cannot digest, and all the things mentioned in the poem have been found, at one time or another, in a shark's stomach.

*Page 17*  CRABS are members of the Crustacean family, with jointed limbs, two pair of antennae, and a hard shell that protects its body. Crabs range from microscopic animals to the 12-foot giant spider crabs of Japan. Most—but not all—crabs scuttle sideways rather than walk forward and back.

*Page 19*  PORTUGUESE MAN-OF-WAR is not one animal, but rather a colony of small animals in a single group, and organized as to their special functions. It has long tentacles that hang down from a central body, or float, which slightly resembles the helmets Portuguese soldiers used to wear, which is how it got its name.

*Page 21*  LEATHERBACK TURTLE is the largest of the sea turtles and is said to be able to swim nearly twenty miles an hour. It has a thick, ridged shell that can often be seen riding above the water. The leatherback can grow very big; average length is between six and eight feet. It can weigh nearly a ton—a surprise, since its diet is mainly jellyfish.

*Page 22*  SALMON journey upstream—even up waterfalls—on their trip to their home mating grounds. They have been known to leap as high as ten feet out of deep water. Bears will wade into the rivers during the salmon runs to catch the leaping silver fish. But it is an extraordinarily tiring journey. After spawning, most of the salmon die. Only about one fish in ten manages to make the trip back down the rivers to the ocean with the young salmon.

*Page 24*  SEA OTTER is the most recent mammal to go back to the sea and become wholly marine. In the past, sea otters were hunted almost to extinction for their fur. One of the most fascinating things about the sea otters is their range of vocal tones, each with a specific meaning, as noted in the poem.

*Page 27*  OCTOPUSES belong to the group of animals known as molluscs, or "soft-bodied animals." In other words, they have no backbones. Surrounding an octopus' mouth are eight long, flexible arms with either a single or a double row of suckers. Those arms can be useful in any number of ways.

*Page 28-29*  BARRACUDA is a pikelike fish with long, pointed jaws filled with razored teeth. *Picuda*, the great barracuda, is thought by some to be even more dangerous than a shark. Barracuda approach without fear of anything that moves in the water.

*Page 30*  KILLER WHALES are actually toothed whales, and the largest of the dolphin family. They can grow up to thirty feet long and weigh as much as eight tons. Though they are the handsome acrobats of the aquarium shows, in the ocean they move in packs and attack like wolves, surrounding their prey and biting off pieces until they kill it. They will attack fish, seals, birds, and even other whales twenty times their size.